AF538271

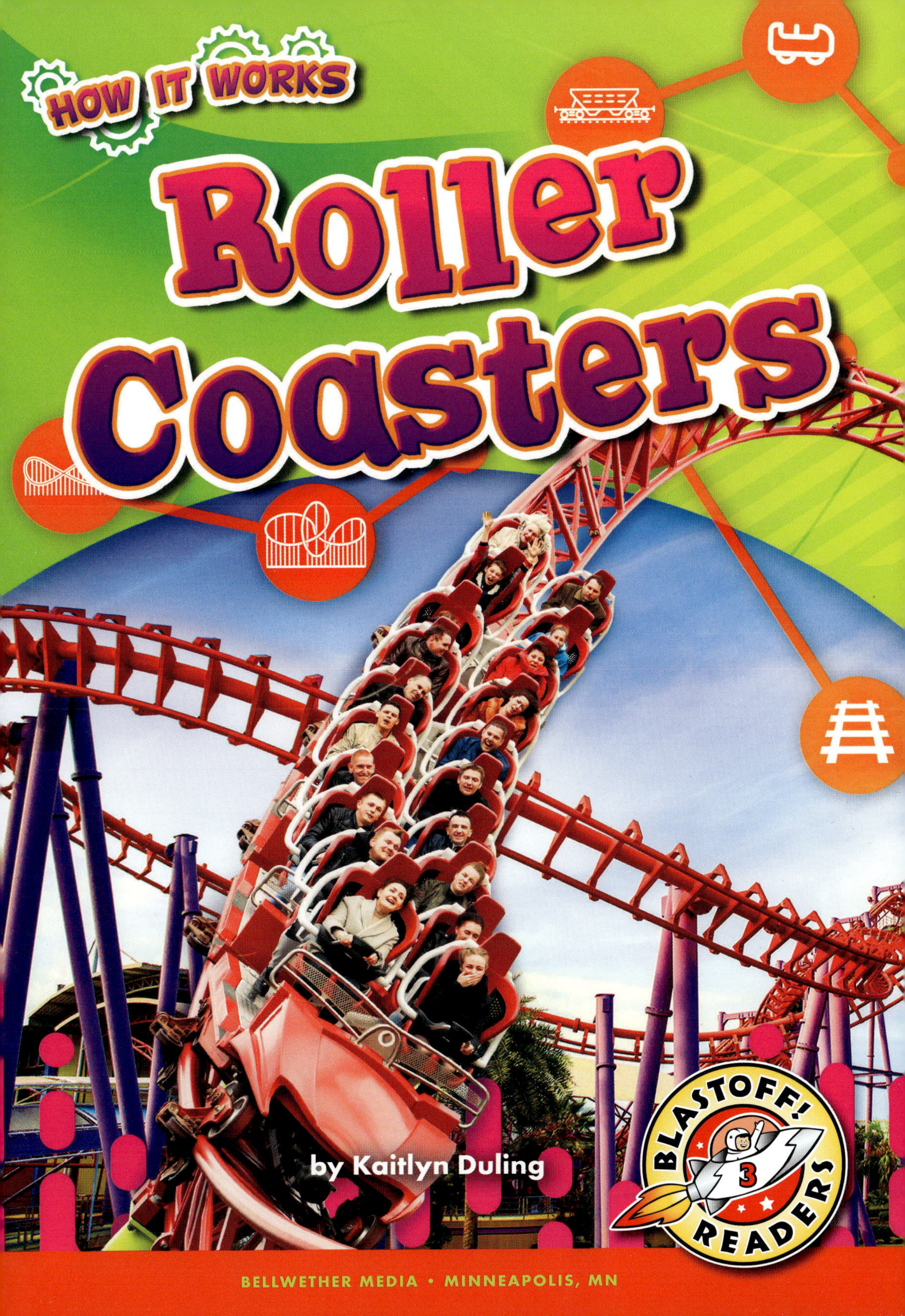
HOW IT WORKS
Roller Coasters
by Kaitlyn Duling
BLASTOFF! READERS
3
BELLWETHER MEDIA • MINNEAPOLIS, MN

Blastoff! Readers are carefully developed by literacy experts to build reading stamina and move students toward fluency by combining standards-based content with developmentally appropriate text.

Level 1 provides the most support through repetition of high-frequency words, light text, predictable sentence patterns, and strong visual support.

Level 2 offers early readers a bit more challenge through varied sentences, increased text load, and text-supportive special features.

Level 3 advances early-fluent readers toward fluency through increased text load, less reliance on photos, advancing concepts, longer sentences, and more complex special features.

★ **Blastoff! Universe**

Reading Level

Blastoff! Beginners — Grade K → Blastoff! Readers — Grades 1–3 → Blastoff! Discovery — Grade 4

This edition first published in 2023 by Bellwether Media, Inc.

Library of Congress Cataloging-in-Publication Data

LC record for Roller Coasters available at: https://lccn.loc.gov/2022020069

Editor: Rachael Barnes   Series Design: Jeffrey Kollock   Book Designer: Josh Brink

Printed in the United States of America, North Mankato, MN.

Table of Contents

What Are Roller Coasters?

Roller coasters are rides that carry people. They go up, down, and around. Some go upside down!

Roller coasters have cars that form a train. Trains move on tracks made of wood or steel.

How Do Roller Coasters Work?

At the start of a ride, a **cable** connects to the bottom of the train. A **motor** pulls the cable.

The train climbs high! **Potential energy** builds as it goes up the **lift hill**.

lift hill

At the top of the lift hill, the cable stops pulling. The train speeds down the hill!

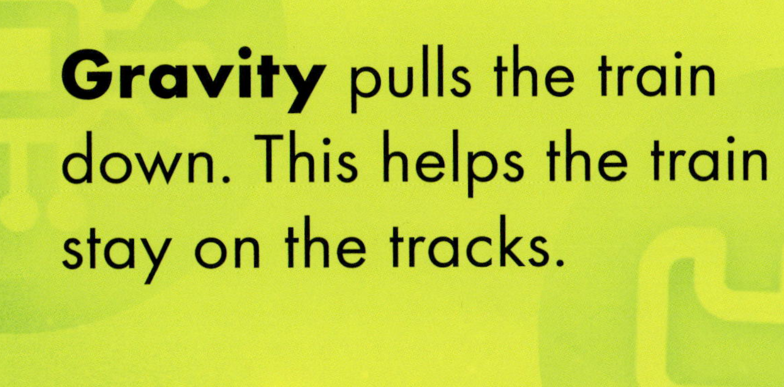

Gravity pulls the train down. This helps the train stay on the tracks.

Parts of A Roller Coaster

car

wheel

tracks

The train gains speed as it rolls downhill. The movement turns the train's potential energy into **kinetic energy**.

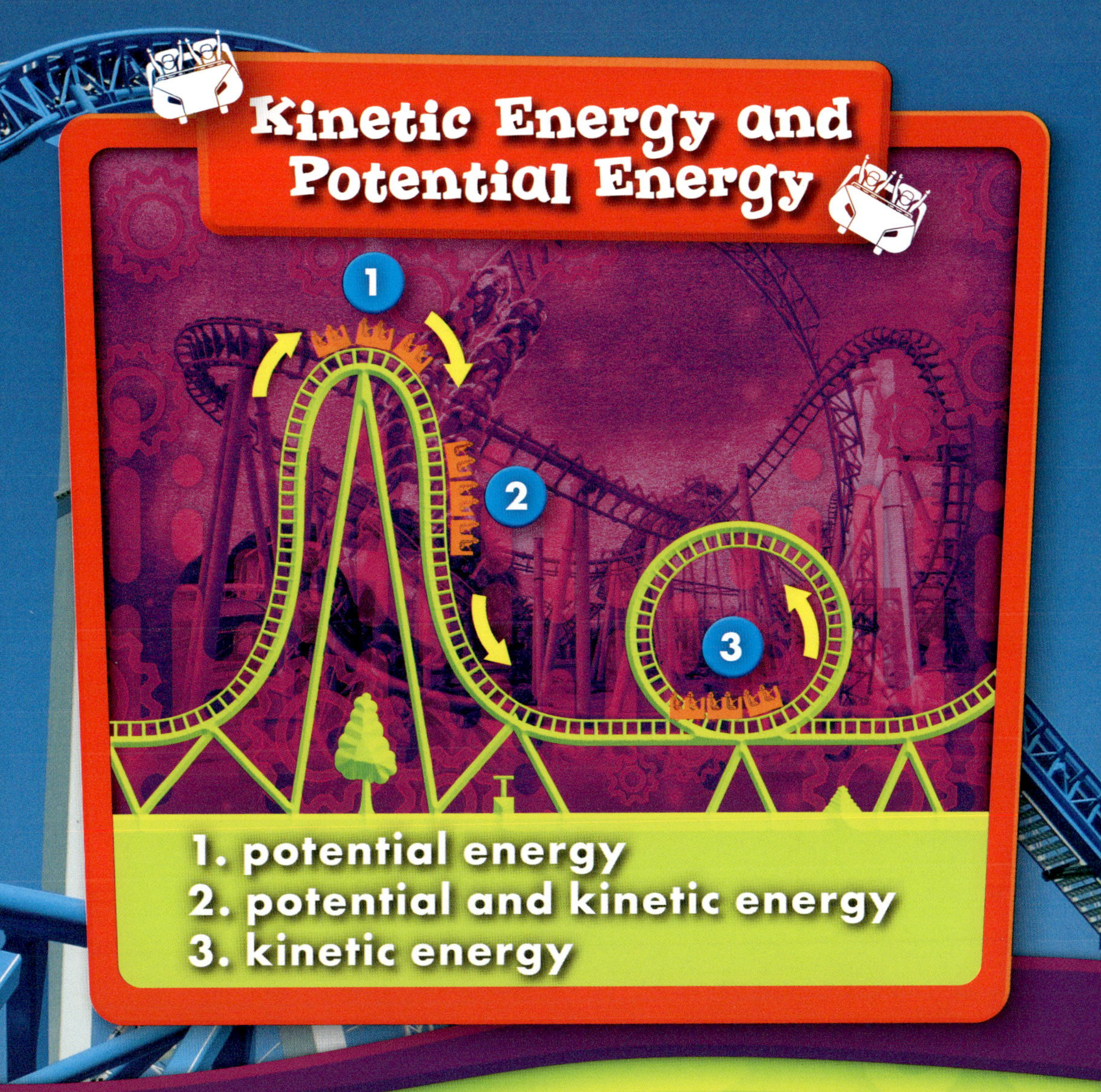

The kinetic energy pushes the train up the next hill. The train moves between potential and kinetic energy on every hill.

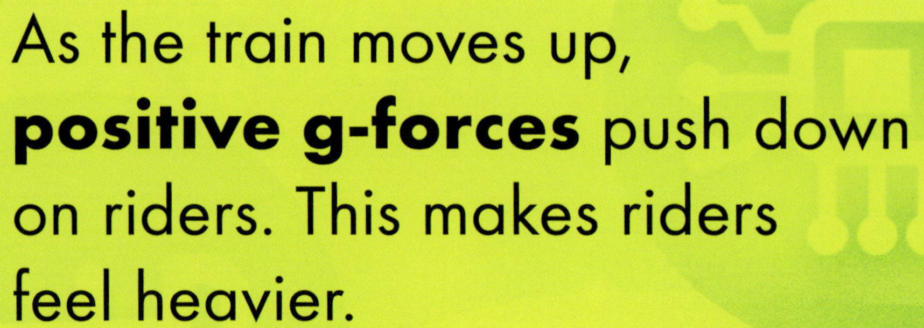

As the train moves up, **positive g-forces** push down on riders. This makes riders feel heavier.

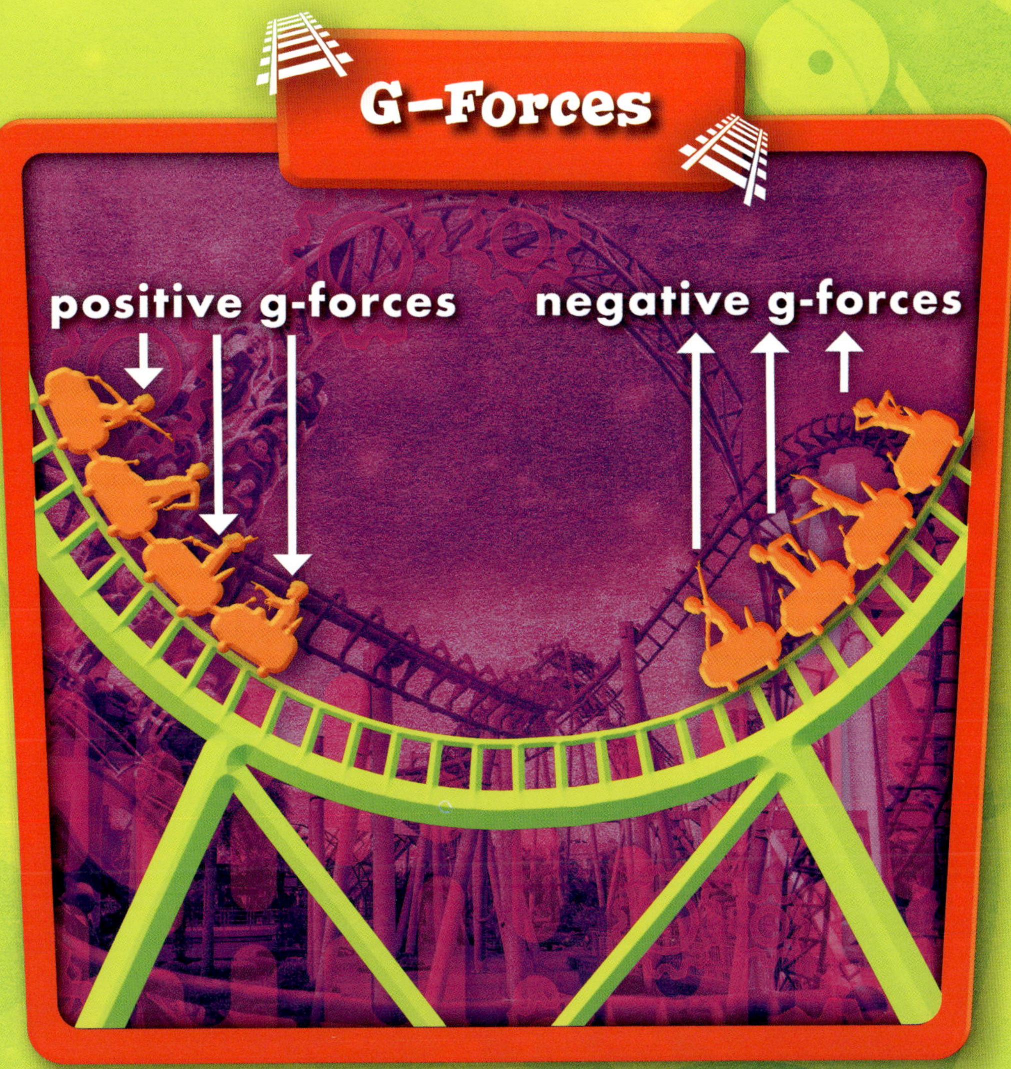

Going down steep hills makes riders feel weightless. They feel like they are floating! This is caused by **negative g-forces**.

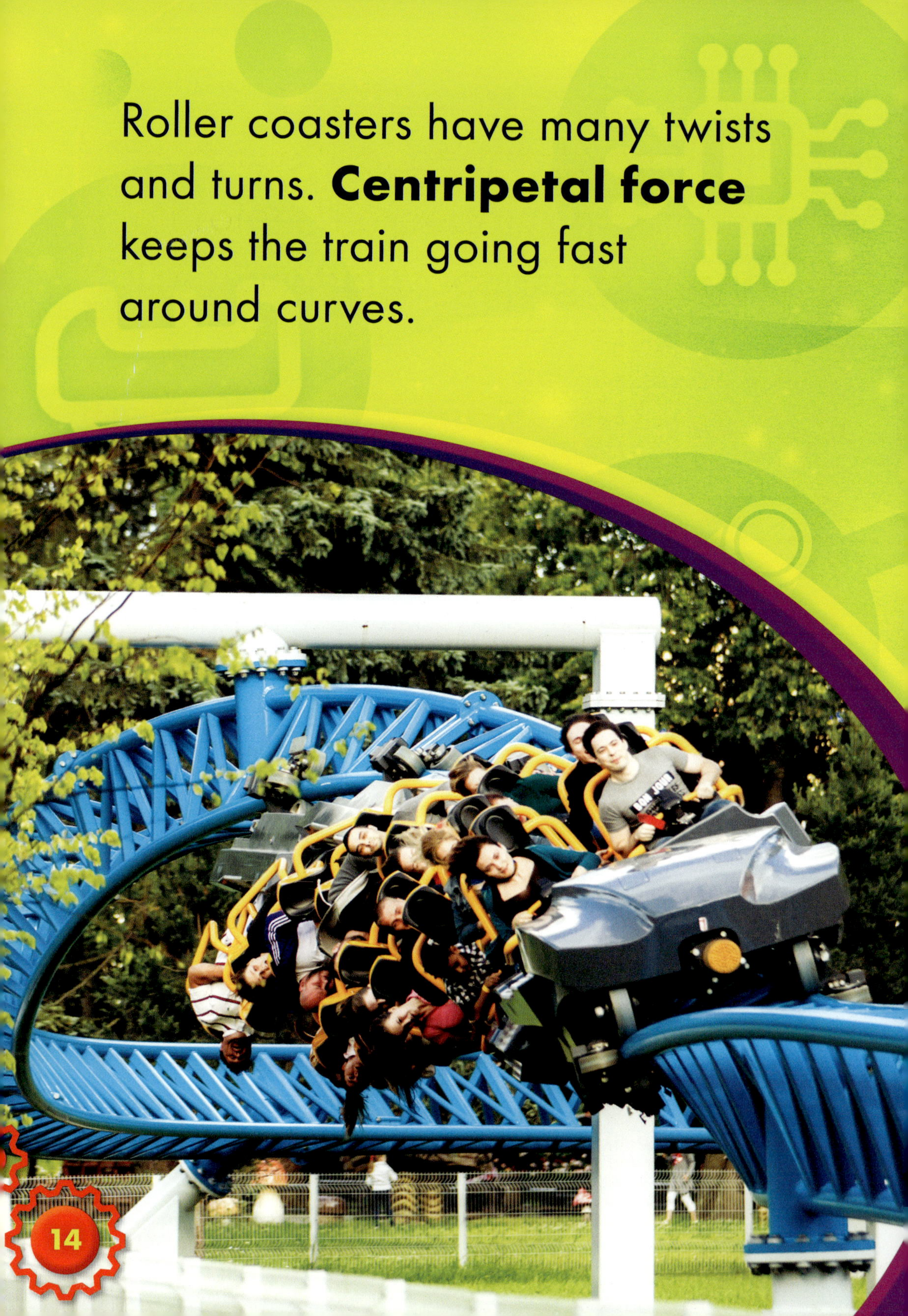

Roller coasters have many twists and turns. **Centripetal force** keeps the train going fast around curves.

Riders may be pushed to the left or right. They feel **lateral forces** as the train turns.

As the train moves, its wheels rub on the tracks. This creates **friction**.

Friction causes the train to slow down. Brakes help the train come to a stop. The riders can safely exit!

The Future of Roller Coasters

Many roller coaster fans love new and surprising rides. Some rides are offering **virtual reality** headsets.

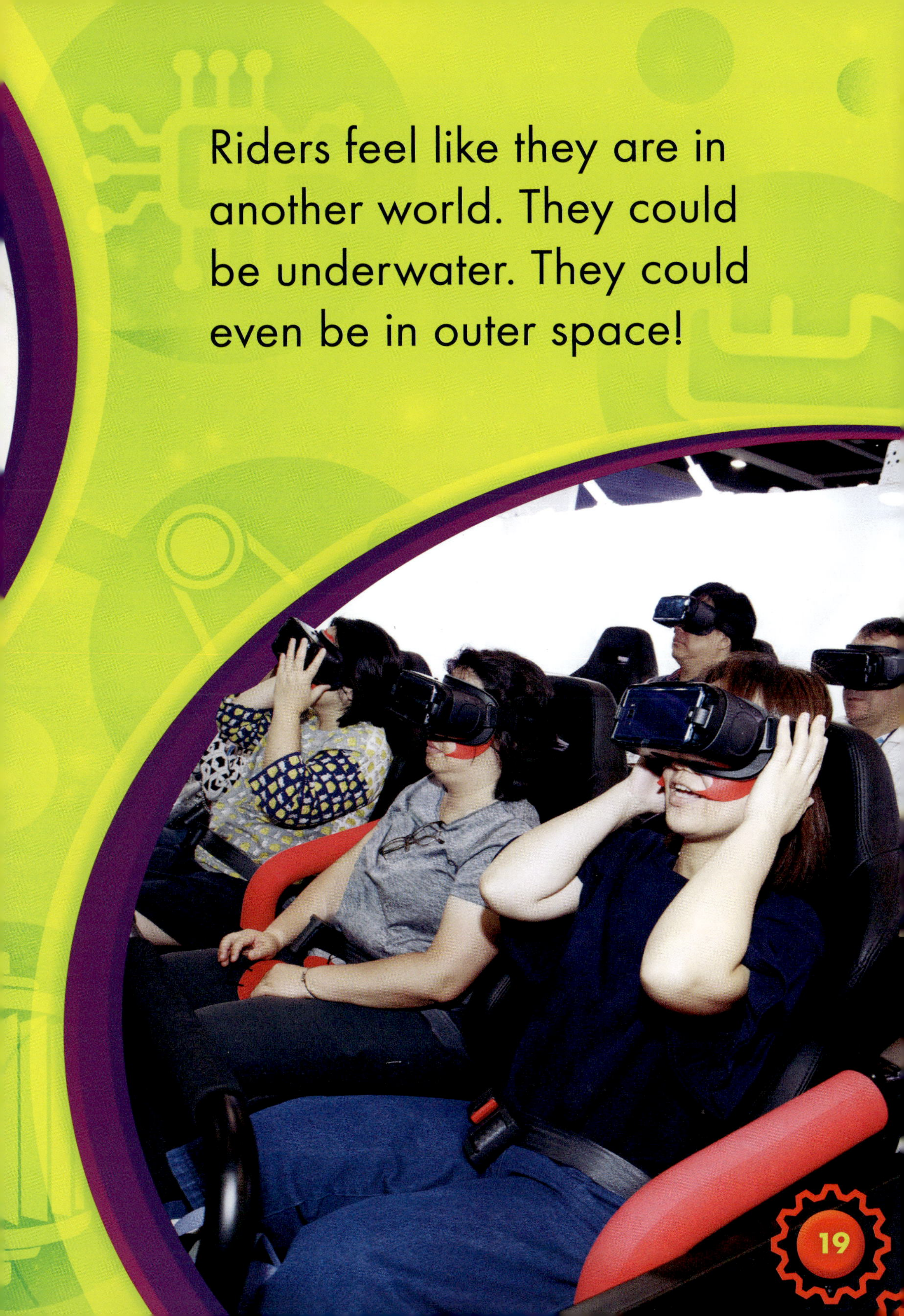

Riders feel like they are in another world. They could be underwater. They could even be in outer space!

Someday, roller coasters may not have wheels. Instead, they could float above powerful **magnets**.

Question

If you could design a roller coaster, what would it look like?

Whatever they look like, roller coasters of the future are sure to make us scream!

Glossary

cable—a thick, strong rope, wire, or chain

centripetal force—a force that keeps an object moving in a curved path

friction—the force created when two things rub against each other; friction slows down moving objects.

gravity—a force that pulls objects toward other objects; Earth's gravity pulls people toward the ground.

kinetic energy—moving energy; roller coasters gain kinetic energy when they speed down drops.

lateral forces—forces that pull objects side-to-side

lift hill—the first and highest hill on a roller coaster

magnets—metals that can pull other metals toward them

motor—a machine that causes something to move

negative g-forces—gravitational forces that create a sense of weightlessness

positive g-forces—gravitational forces that create a sense of heaviness

potential energy—stored energy; roller coasters have potential energy at the tops of hills.

virtual reality—related to a type of computer program that makes users feel like they are in a different place

To Learn More

AT THE LIBRARY

Amin, Anita Nahta. *Amazing Roller Coasters.* Minneapolis, Minn.: Jump!, 2023.

Bowman, Chris. *Roller Coasters.* Minneapolis, Minn.: Bellwether Media, 2019.

Mikoley, Kate. *How a Roller Coaster Is Built.* New York, N.Y.: Gareth Stevens Publishing, 2020.

ON THE WEB

FACTSURFER

Factsurfer.com gives you a safe, fun way to find more information.

1. Go to www.factsurfer.com.
2. Enter "roller coasters" into the search box and click 🔍.
3. Select your book cover to see a list of related content.

Index

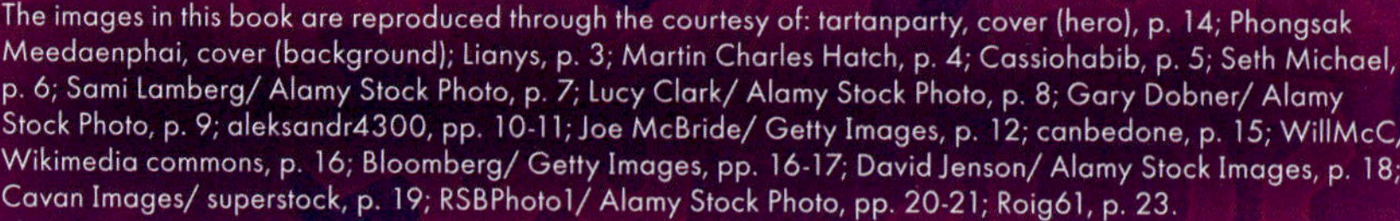

The images in this book are reproduced through the courtesy of: tartanparty, cover (hero), p. 14; Phongsak Meedaenphai, cover (background); Lianys, p. 3; Martin Charles Hatch, p. 4; Cassiohabib, p. 5; Seth Michael, p. 6; Sami Lamberg/ Alamy Stock Photo, p. 7; Lucy Clark/ Alamy Stock Photo, p. 8; Gary Dobner/ Alamy Stock Photo, p. 9; aleksandr4300, pp. 10-11; Joe McBride/ Getty Images, p. 12; canbedone, p. 15; WillMcC/ Wikimedia commons, p. 16; Bloomberg/ Getty Images, pp. 16-17; David Jenson/ Alamy Stock Images, p. 18; Cavan Images/ superstock, p. 19; RSBPhoto1/ Alamy Stock Photo, pp. 20-21; Roig61, p. 23.